# The Monster Book of Witches Vampires Spooks and ( Monsters )

## Colin & Jacqui Hawkins

Colour Library Direct

# Witches

Pointed hat ➞

weRd

Rare Black Ferret, very powerful talisman against pick pockets.

Raven

Long black gown

foraging pram.

foragjno

# Which is Witch?

According to ancient writings,

'A witch be known by her great age, wrinkled face, furrowed brow, hairy lip, gober teeth, squint eye, squeaking voice, scolding tongue, ragged coat and the cat or dog by her side.'

This is, of course, a very good description of lots of people, especially grannies, and even more especially of old grannies. Even if your granny has all these qualities, it still doesn't mean that she is a witch. Watch for other signs. Ask yourself these questions:

1. Has your granny a fondness for wearing long black gowns and tall pointed hats?
2. Does she cook weeds, roots and herbs in enormous black pots?
3. Does your granny like to dance round the garden at midnight? If so, does she dance *a)* alone, *b)* with her cronies, *c)* only at full moon, *d)* at other times?
4. Can your granny raise storms at sea, call up the wind, bring rain?
5. Does your granny fly? If so, does she fly *a)* on her broomstick, *b)* on the back of her cat, *c)* on an aeroplane?
6. Can your granny change her shape? Have you ever seen her as *a)* a butterfly, *b)* a raven, *c)* a spider?
7. Can your granny cure *a)* fevers, *b)* agues, *c)* bad humours?

If you answered yes to any of these questions, your granny is almost certainly a witch. If you answered no to them all, here is one further test you can apply;

Ask your granny if she likes tea. A true witch will answer yes.

If you decide that your granny is definitely a witch, read this book and find out more about the powers and practices of her kind. And be kind to her, witches need a lot of love.

Very wise familiar

A familiar hat

Familiar atop a familiar

A furry familiar

A familiar smile

Suspended familiar

A familiar pair

Spotted familiar

# Looks Familiar

If you are talking behind your granny's back, make sure her cat is not listening. For her cat is probably not a real cat at all. It is probably her familiar, an imp that has taken the form of a cat. Familiars are used by witches to gather information and gossip. They take messages to other witches. They help to gather ingredients for spells and generally make themselves useful.

Not all familiars are cats, of course. They can be dogs, birds, toads, crocodiles and even spiders, but cats are most popular because they can forecast the weather and help a witch to change it. Watch your granny's cat. If it claws at the carpet or at the curtains, it is raising the wind. If it washes its ears or sneezes, rain will come.

Though familiars are a great help to a witch and good company, they often become too familiar. Cats will often walk all over their witch. The expression 'familiarity breeds contempt' comes from this habit.

"Watch the birdie".

An over familiar familiar.

Weathercocks are a protection against the powers of darkness.

Beware of bats in the hair.

13

To be near an elder tree or witch oak after dusk is to run the risk of being placed in the power of witches.

Beware of cats that stare.

Broomstick shed.

# Home Sour Home

Witches tend to live in houses of great age, but it is not always easy to tell a witch's house for certain. Signs to look for are: an unlucky number on the door; a very slender garage; multiple cat flaps; blackened windows; a weather vane blowing backwards; a witch answering the door. If you suspect that a house belongs to a witch (unless it is your granny's) do not go too close. You could become bewitched.

Inside, the witch's house is well furnished, with moulted cat-fur carpets, raven flock wallpaper and cobweb curtains at the windows. Upstairs, the bedrooms contain beds, baskets, bees' nests, perches, crocodile cots and cats' cradles.

Witches are often called out at night to cast spells or perform a bit of hocus pocus, so they have to snatch what sleep they can, snoozing in an easy chair or dozing in front of the television. Some people believe that witches never sleep at all. Ask your granny if she sleeps well.

You will notice that witches never have newspapers delivered to their homes. Stale news is of no interest to them. They prefer to read the future in the flames of the fire. Books are another matter. A witch needs a good library of recipe books and spellbooks, and notebooks for writing up new spells. Not only bookworms will be found in the library but book caterpillars, book beetles and book spiders – even the odd bookfrog will slide along the shelves.

Bats
hate
water

Baths
are rarely
if ever a
private
affair.

Soap wort
lather.

A familiar cat
scrubbing a familiar back.

# Hubble Bubble Bath

Contrary to popular belief, witches like to wash or bath every day, and most wash and curl their hair at least once a week. Bubbles are a must. Soapwort leaves, bruised, tied in muslin, and agitated with water produce a luxurious foam in minutes. To create an especially soothing bath after a hectic night, many witches add lavender to the water, a favourite witch scent. See if your granny likes lavender.

Bathtime is also beauty time, with extra care given to hair and complexion. Secret health and beauty recipes are handed down from witch mother to witch daughter. Ointments, herbs, lotions, shampoos, powders and scents, all combine to give the characteristically sleek shiny locks and soft downy skin of a young witch. Lips are polished and fangs varnished.

The problem of over familiar familiars often becomes acute at bathtime.

Bath water thrown over leeks will encourage hardy growth.

The normal height
of a witch is
between 1·5
and 3 metres
(including hat.)

Night Light Hat.
complete with
funnel and
snuffer.
used for
reading in
bed. and on
moonless nights

Hat brim
can be
folded down
and tied
over the ears
in cold weather.

Black
vest →

Open
finger
mittens

Portable
cauldron

— Secret pockets

Liberty
Bodice →

Winter
warmth
bloomers.

Black
stretch
stockings

Stout leather boots

# Witch Wear

Witches are old fashioned in their choice of clothes. They believe that their garments should be hard wearing and good value for money. Clothes should be warm for chilly October flights and reasonably waterproof, especially during June rain bottling. They need to be of a colour that will not show cauldron splashes or garden grubbings.

Most important, clothes should be comfortable, allowing complete freedom of movement for arm waving and leg jerking spells. The classic witch gown has extra deep pockets for keeping such witch essentials as sandwiches, tea flasks, safety pins, string, old stockings, toads and knicker elastic.

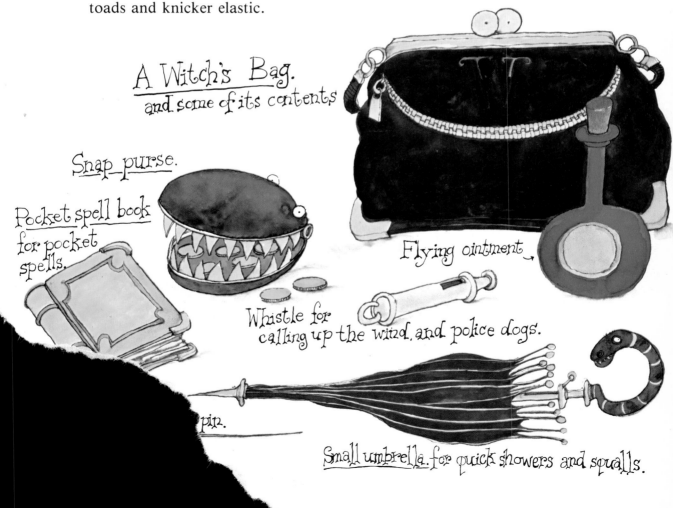

A Witch's Bag.
and some of its contents

Snap purse.

Pocket spell book for pocket spells.

Flying ointment.

Whistle for calling up the wind and police dogs.

pin.

Small umbrella for quick showers and squalls.

# Snap Cackle Pop

A prune
a day
makes
witches
gay.

A breakfast of
ant eggs eaten
raw, will restore
the senses.

Pains
in the belly
can be cured
by jelly

Bats will rarely, if ever get up in time for b

Dropping
in for
breakfast

Second
helpings

Toasted
cheese,
please.

Witches eat heartily at breakfast. Most are especially fond of witch's sago, made from preserved frogspawn. A favourite second course is dawn-gathered toadstools on toast. After that, for the sour toothed, there is delicious sloe jam, with acorn bread and steaming hot dandelion coffee. In the old days, witches had to cast a spell to sour their milk, but nowadays sour cream can be easily had from the supermarket.

Not so with food for the familiars; very few shops stock tinned toad food, raven seed, batburgers or choice cuts for crocodiles. So breakfast can take a long time, even with an imaginative witch at the stove. And with so many to feed it's not surprising that the cupboard is soon bare.

A cat on the mat
is a cat that is
fat.

...And when the cupboard is bare...

The spell to make the bus come.

Note use of thumb.

Sometimes this spell can be too strong.

# Shock in Store

Whistling up sausages.

Ninety per cent of butchers say that they can recognize a witch in their shop.

Only the stalest bread will do for a really fussy witch.

French bread should wrapped before leaving the bakery.

Year candle.

Candle stick maker

Since the invention of electricity, witches have been more welcome at the candlestickmakers.

In times gone by, a witch had to trail from shop to shop for her provisions. Today she can shop in half the time and with twice the fun. The supermarket has become a great centre for witches meeting, exchanging news, gossip and the latest spells, and taking part in the weekly race to the check out. It is worth noting that witches like to shop between 5.30 and 7.00pm on Friday evenings – a time to avoid supermarkets if at all possible.

not a witch

# Green Fingers

Few shops stock the variety of ingredients that a witch needs constantly at hand for her spells. So a witch must cultivate her garden, keeping the ground free from flowers that choke the weeds, and clearing mushrooms from space where nettles and toadstools could grow.

Because witches can hear a plant in pain, they are careful to cast plant sleeping spells before cutting a single stem. No crying creepers, shrieking violets, mournful moss or wisteria with hysteria will be found in a witch's garden. Nor will you find plants tied to stakes or forced to stand in rows against the wall.

Favourite witch plants are nettles, dandelions, the tastier toadstools, ground elder, chickweed, rosemary, foxgloves, cucumbers and roses. See if your granny has any of these plants in her garden.

Hollyhocks: a good remedy for spongy gums.

Cucumbers, pumpkins,
cress and claws
Will soothe a nose that is
covered in sores

A welcome crow

To stay in fine
fettle,
eat a
nettle

Dandelions
Will induce restful
sleep rarely.

Chickweed
A cure for itch
and scabs.

Not much room
for mushrooms

One or two drops of bats blood, mixed with deadly night shade, foxglove and the grease of a boar, make an excellent flying ointment.

'A moth in the broth will cure your cough.'

It is thought that there are more witch cures for warts than there are warts in the world.

'Toe nails, that are grown long are useful to bind a spell strong.'

# Spelling Lessons

Throughout the centuries people have feared witches. In a trice, one of these old crones might transform you into a cat or a toadstool or a bat, or even, if you are a prince, into a frog. Now, there is no doubt that some witches have a nastier side to their magic, a little bit of mischief here, a little bit of hocum there. But, on the whole, witches have usually practised their arts to good purpose. Worn out by the toil and trouble of slaving over a hot cauldron, many witches have grown old before their time, just trying to help ordinary people.

To make an active potion, the witch needs not only the right mixture, cooked at the exact temperature, but she also needs to know the precise form of words for casting the spell.

This involves a young witch in hours of tedious practice after school. She must take cookery lessons, study recipes, learn shorthand and typing and millions of chants, calls, shrieks, mutters and incantations. Without a good grounding in spelling, a witch cannot hope for a successful career.

The simplest spells deal with the weather. To raise a storm at sea, for instance, a witch merely has to swing a cat three times round her head and then throw it into the sea, chanting,

'Screech, screech, screech and scraw,
Make the sea rage and roar.'

More difficult but more worthwhile are spells for curing ailments.

Successful rainmaking witch.

Dry toad.

# Kill or Cupe

If you have warts, try these cures: Place in a bag as many pebbles as you have warts and leave the bag at a crossroads. The warts will be transferred to whoever picks up the bag. Or, prick your warts with a pin and stick the pin into an ash tree, reciting: 'Ashen tree, ashen tree, pray take away these warts from me.' If your warts do not transfer to the tree, ask your granny what to do.

Warts
The bag and pebbles method.

As a cure for tooth ache a dead mole should be worn around the neck.

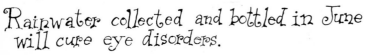

Rainwater collected and bottled in June will cure eye disorders.

You and your family may like to try these cures and spells.

If you have tummy ache, stand on your head for two minutes and say 'Ickle, dickle, dockle day, Take this horrid pain away.'

If you have a cough, stay in bed and take owl broth three times a day.

If you have a toothache, wear a dead mole around your neck.

If you have fever, take pills of compressed spiders' webs before breakfast.

If you have sore knees, boil up some cabbage and some caterpillars with some chocolate sponge and eat the mixture at bedtime.

If you have a runny nose, hold your ears and touch your toes.

If a dog bites you, take some hair of the dog, fry it and place it on the wound together with a sprig of rosemary.

Boar's grease cures Gout
Greasy boars are not easy to find and so should be allowed to drive the bath chair occasionally

If your head aches, close your eyes, stay very still and count silently to a hundred. This cure may have to be tried over and over again before it works. And even if it doesn't work on your headache, it may cure granny's.

The cure for a dog bite

# Friendship

Witches like to get together. Coffee mornings, whist drives, coach outings, tennis tournaments and tea parties are all good excuses for a cosy gossip. For entertainment after a tea party the witches watch television or tell each other's fortune in the tea leaves (witches never use tea bags). Tea being drunk, each witch passes her cup to the left. The witch next to her swirls it three times in her left hand before draining off the dregs. Patterns near the handle represent the near future, those in the upper part more distant events and those in the bottom the very distant future. Patterns shaped like crosses, spades, guns, snakes, cats or toads spell bad luck; moonshapes, clover leaves, flowers, trees, crows and the number seven foretell good luck. See if you can tell fortunes this way. Ask you granny to help you at first.

After a supper party, witches like to dance, practising the latest steps and listening to the top ten, ready for the big witch festivals. Finding suitable partners is often a problem for witches.

A witched kettle never boils.

A slow kettle could be bewitched and contain a toad.

ches.

A flight or cackle of Witches

# Flying High

Goats can be flown if no other choice is available.

Ancient texts tell of skies black with witches flying to the Sabbath and loud with screeching and cackling. But broomstick flying is dangerous, cold and uncomfortable so most witches prefer to travel by bus, bicycle or car. In fact, they usually only fly to important witch gatherings such as Sabbaths or Halloween, or in cases of public transport strikes or great emergency.

Witches traditionally fly on broomsticks, though sometimes they use cats, cockerels, horses, large dogs or, if really desperate, goats. A horse found in the morning, tired, sweating and not fit for work might well have been hag ridden during the night. On witch Sabbaths, farmers guard their stables to stop their horses being stolen.

Riding to the Sabbath.

Before take off, the witch must rub flying ointment all over her body.
The smell of this mixture of bat's blood, deadly nightshade, foxglove
juice and boar's grease is a sure sign that a witch will be flying tonight.

Shape changing into a bird, fly or other flying creature is a short cut
to flying. Witches can change themselves into any creature they wish,
from ants to weasels, though cats and hares are the most popular choice.
A witch is usually unable to change into a dove or a white rabbit.

Shape Shifting
Cats and hares are the
most popular form taken,
and occasionally
flies.

Shape changing
into doves was
never successful.

# High Jinks

The witches' year begins at Halloween, a time when ghosts demons and children roam abroad demanding treats or offering tricks. Homes are decorated with candles in turnips and pumpkins with faces; apples are bobbed and bonfires burnt.

Dancing the traditional Beltane, Knee's up Mother Brown.

To dance the Widdershins, (the dance of the witches) form a circle 3·5 m in diameter around a bonfire and dance in the opposite direction to that of the sun's path around the sky.

On Halloween the witches gather at midnight and dance flush-cheeked around the flames until dawn. Round and round the bonfire, dancing widdershins, waltzing, quickstepping, slowstepping, sidestepping, twisting, shaking and just doing their thing. No other festival lives up to Halloween for fashions, flying and fun.

Candlemas, for instance, is a time for cleanliness and goodliness. Witches burn candles as a sign of their purity.

On Valentine's Day, young witches place bay leaves under their pillows in order to dream of their future husbands. It is not known how accurate their dreams are.

Beltane celebrates the start of summer and is time for more high jinks. Young witches dance round the maypole, hoping to attract enough attention to be chosen Queen of the May.

If a young witch has not found a husband by Beltane, she can try again around the Midsummer's Eve bonfire.

At the harvest festival of Lammas, a girl has her last chance. Often witches bake magic cakes with the newly harvested corn to offer to their sweethearts. If they cannot charm a man with their charms, they will charm him with their spells.

Some needed more purification than others.

With Bay leaves under her pillow, a girl will dream of her future husband.

The first loaf of Lammas.

A coven of witches usually consists of 13 witches.

toad.

This coven is playing the ancient game of pass the toad.

# Witch Facts?

A favourite spell of witches and wizards is to turn a Prince into a frog, or Rover into a toad.

If you want to know the way ask an old witch.

Witches have been known to live to a great age some well beyond 65 years.

An old witch in her later years will teach all she knows to a young novice witch.

Many witches practise great skill in the art of broomstick flying.

In ancient times both male and female witches were often said to have the ability to worry sheep.

another worried sheep.

C Two worried sheep.

Misunderstood black cat →

Witches are very fond of cats, especially black cats. They are the most popular choice as familiars and, like witches, have long been misunderstood.

Twins especially witch twins, have long been thought to possess unique powers.

Although also regarded by many to be double trouble.

The words printed above this line are in a secret language that only
witches can see. Ask your granny what they say.

# Vampires

Vampires

# The Curse of the Vampire

Neither living nor dead, the vampire is a creature of the night.
It steals through the darkness to prey on humankind, to drain
them of their life's blood. And when the exhausted victims die,
they in their turn become the 'undead'.

For centuries ordinary people have tried to rid the world of
vampires, pursuing them with mirrors, garlic, sick pigs, sour
milk, Christmas puddings, wooden stakes and ever more
ingenious weapons. But, as fast as a new remedy is devised, it is
proved useless against the supernatural cunning of the evil ones
who walk by night.

Typical 19th Century
Vampire lair on
bleak Transylvanian
hillside.

# The Living Dead

You can recognize a vampire by its gaunt appearance and deathly pale complexion. Look for its full red lips, pointed canine teeth and gleaming hypnotic eyes. Notice the long sharp finger-nails and eyebrows that meet in the middle. Look for hairs in the palm of the hand and watch out for anyone who chooses to sleep in a coffin. Take care – even your best friend could be a vampire.

# Vampires Today

## Evening Dress
Vampire bats and werewolves are easily recognisable by their dinner suits.

## Vampire Chant
Lock your windows
Close your doors
No one is safe from
Our fangs and
claws.

cold wet nose

Cold wet nose, glossy coat and bright eyes are signs of a happy and well nourished werewolf.

A short whiskered, dribbling wolf in a bow tie and dinner jacket is certain to be a vampire.

Vampires can live for hundreds of years, so long as they get plenty of rest – and blood. Not that being dead and alive is easy. Shape changing, for example – into wolves, bats, dogs, evening dress – is very wearing but often practised.

Watch out for wolves, bats, dogs and men in evening dress. And listen at night for moths pinging at your window, owls hooting, cats howling. They could be servants of a vampire – watching you.

Beware of owls on the prowl and moths that cough.

'cough!'

'cough!'

Old vampires are especially fond of Bat-en-berg cake.

♬ Happy Birthday ♬    Dear Igor    Happy ♬ Birthday to you.

# Vampires Around the World

Once vampires lived only in Eastern Europe; today they live in many other parts of the world. Different nationalities have different characteristics. The Bavarian vampire, for instance, sleeps with one eye open and its thumbs linked. British vampires read The Times and carry black umbrellas. See if there is one in your street.

The Bulgarian Vampire has only one nostril.

only one nostril

The Transylvanian vampire has a passion for high heels and old ladies.

"what a drag"

"'tis a fine night for a bite"

Irish Vampires hate the taste of blood.

Paddy Von Blutto.

# Vampire Lore

A vampire at night is an awful sight
And his bite will give you
a terrible fright.

According to ancient texts vampires will crumble to dust if caught in the rays of the sun. So, if you wake to find a vampire leaning over you, don't panic, just try to keep it talking until dawn.

Another remedy is to eat as much garlic as you can and breathe over the creature until it flees back to its grave.

A hole by a grave is a sure sign that it is occupied by a vampire. But neither boiling water nor smoke will disturb the sleeping tenant.

Garlic breath.

Eeek!

An old trick to make a vampire sick...
Ruby lips with garlic spread will save your neck from being bled.

A grave matter

Stone the crows.

what

'Tis a vampires hole!

Or that of a mole

Into bed you must tumble. Before the dawn. Or you will crumble.
Afore the sun is in the sky..
Be back in bed
Or you will die!

*Vampire Nursery Rhyme*

Ok, stranger - quit hanging around, or I'll fill you full of silver.

"Yup. and quit sucking blood out of people's ears!"

coo!

The only sure way of exterminating a vampire is to drive a stake through its heart while it sleeps – not easy with the Bavarian!

In America a silver bullet may be shot through the heart, though American vampires don't hang about for long.

A simple method of slaying a British vampire is to steal the umbrella and thrust it into its heart. If the vampire is reading its paper, it will hardly notice.

# Vampires at Work

"I'll soon have a nice hole drilled in that Sir."

**N**owadays, vampires lead relatively normal lives, coping with all but the brightest sunlight. Vampires are found in all walks of life.

**T**here are vampire bus drivers, vampire lollypop ladies, vampire teachers, vampire shopkeepers, vampire traffic wardens, vampire doctors, vampire butchers, vampire tax collectors and, the most popular choice of all, vampire undertakers.

## A Vampire Astronaut.

"Did you know that in space no one can hear you scream?"

# Vampire Doctors.

I do not like thee, Doctor Drac,
and certainly not behind
my back ...

(Part of old chant.)

"Open
wide
and
pop it
inside."

# Vampire Undertakers.

♪ Be it in May, or
on a cold winter's day.
In a coffin one day. We'll
take you away. ♪

( Traditional Undertakers' grave song. )

# Family Life

\* Note for scholars
Bluot is old high
German for blood.

The Von Bluots\* are a typical vampire family. They are descended from
a proud and ancient family of Bavarian vampires but now live in Bradford.

Like most other British families, their day begins with a warming breakfast –
a nourishing bowl of bones for all. After a quick skim through The
Times, Vlad the Dad sees the children off to school and drives to his job as a
civil servant. At four o'clock in the afternoon he is free to pursue his favourite
sport – coffin jogging. Vlad is the local champ and is training for the marathon.

"Hurry up
and eat your
soup dear,
before
it clots"

# At Home
# with Mother

At home, Mum – Mrs Belladonna
Plasma Von Bluot – looks after baby
Wallachia. The baby is nine months
old, very happy, very wicked and
very healthy. She has just grown her
first fang. Her full name is
Wallachia Julie Andrews Von
Bluot, the family having just seen
The Sound of Music for the seventh
time when she was born.

After lunch, Mum takes the baby to
visit Grandpa and Grandma.

A visit to the graveyard.

Say hello to Grandpa
Vlad the Mad Von Bluot.

Goo.

Visiting Granny.

In the evening, the family take a walk in the park with their pets. Vlad the Lad has a dog called Blod and a crow called Carone. His sister Valhalla has a cat called Bloth. Bloth and Blod are constantly at each other's throats but all else is hunky-gory. Young Vlad reads horror comics to Carone; Val nurses her dolls; their parents feed the bats and talk about old times and the children's progress at school. Vlad has been bad again, sent off at rugby for biting in the scrum. But Val has come top in woodwork for making a sweet little coffin for her dolls.

# Goremet Supper

Tonight Valhalla has brought two schoolfriends home for supper.
Despite everybody making them very welcome, the visitors are very quiet
and hardly eat a thing. They cannot even finish their soup.

Vlad the Dad, who 'hasn't had a bite all day,' sinks his teeth into the best end of neck and tries to encourage them. 'Eat up, my dears, the food will make you strong and put hairs on your palms.'

'Come along,' says Mum, 'eat up your soup. Then we'll all have some jelly belly and cream and you can go and play with your bats in the attic.'

# Gory Bedtime Story

Like most other children, the Von Bluots like stories about monsters and mysteries, princes and wizards, goblins and ghouls. But most of all they love to hear about their ancestors. 'Tell us about Vlad the Impaler,' they implore at bedtime, 'and how Vlad the Glad got his fang out in time. Tell us how Vlad the Mad caught Vlad the Cad in Granny's casket. Tell us about Dracula the filmstar . . .'

'That's enough now, dears,' says Mum. 'Settle down and I'll read you a nice grim story by your uncles Jakob and Wilhelm Grimm Von Bluot.'

Bat mobile.

Vampire potty.

"And then the monsters gobbled everyone up and lived happily ever after."

And she reads them not just one tale but four, which only goes to show what magic vampire mothers are.

## Goldifangs and the Three Bears.

↳ The lovely old story about the little girl who loved porridge and bears' blood.

## Little Red Riding Fangs.

Who, it is said, bit on the head a wolf in Granny's bed.

My, My, Granny what a lovely wet nose you have...

Good Grief! look at those teeth!

# And so to bed...?

When the children are asleep, Mum and Dad watch old vampire movies on the television (there never seems to be anything else on). Afterwards they go upstairs . . .

12 Midnight.
Up the wooden Hill..

11.30 pm.

12.02.

12.02½.

12.03

12.05.

So remember –
if a vampire flies through your window tonight,
don't worry, it's only being friendly.
Don't see red, it only wants to make you a
vampire too.
And there are far worse things to be than
a vampire – and I should know.

When the moon is bright
We'll go out for a bite.
We'll give them a fright
In the middle of the
night.

Goodnight Children.
Sweet Dreams.

# Spooks

# Ghost Guises

Ghosts mostly appear as floppy white sheets. (They are said to materialize). Other spooks take different shapes. These are some you may – or may not – see.

Regular sheet ghosts (wraiths)

Headless spook

Bodiless spook

Several ghosts together are known as a shriek of ghosts.

Terrifying ghost

Terrified ghost

A singing spook.

Headless bodiless spook often mistaken for a cloud

Woooooo oo

Invisible friendly spook

Hello

Dem bones.. Dem bones

Invisible spooks make their presence felt – by booing or blowing or making your flesh creep.

struth!

Invisible unfriendly spook

Well it's not me!

A skelespook

# Spook Species.

Spooks can never change. When they return from the dead to haunt the living, they come as they were in life.
Accompanied by his faithful haggis, a Scottish spook plays his ghastly pipes as he stalks the castle battlements.

Irish Banshee

A miserable creature with bad news to tell.

Oh dear
Oh dear
'tis a terrible ting.. a terrible ting

Screech! Screech!

Howl

Wail Wail Whine.. Whine

Can't see yoo, Jimmy

'Ay the Booa

## The Tartan Torment

The Phantom of the Opera.

Heiaha!

Scandinavian Spooks.

all pulling together
after centuries of pillage and plunder

Aimez-vous
le gâteau?

At the Palace of Versailles,
Marie Antoinette endlessly
offers her crumbling cake to
not so poor tourists.

I 'ave
met my
Waterloo
but....
'as anyone
seen
Josephine?

# Animal Apparitions

Even spiders may be spooks

A'har. Jim lad A'har'

'Ghastly grim and ancient raven' guarding ancient treasure

Cor! Stone the crows! I'm not that bad!

## An Old Sea Dog

Sailors do tell of wild stormy nights when the only sound is that of the tap tapping of an old sea dog on the way to his drinking bowl in the seaport tavern.

# A Famous Phantom.

# The Flying Dutchman

Condemned to sail the seven seas
forever, the Dutchman brings death and
destruction to all who witness the
passing of his ship, so DON'T LOOK
AT THIS PAGE

Dick Turpin, on his famous mare Black Bess, preys on those with full piggy banks at lonely zebra crossings.

The loneliest Roman of them all searches for his legion 2000 years too late.

Another Famous Phantom.

Your piggy or your life.

A totally unknown phantom

Quo vadis?

'Or your sugar lumps'.

Spook horse shoes get a lot of wear.

# Spook Spotting

The lights dim, a freezing draught of air whistles under the unopened door, you hear footsteps coming towards you, nearer, nearer, nearer, the dog whines, the door handle turns and . . . you think you've seen a ghost? Don't kid yourself, it's not that easy. Spooks are no fools. You have to be really smart to spot a spook.

Most spooks are snobs, so don't bother spook spotting in high rise flats or council estates. Go to posh places where there are large old houses.

Typical Elizabethan mansion spook with cur.

'Sit Sirrah!'

Woof!

Remember: You'll never find a spook in a semi.

Heads are frequently carried because of the low ceilings.

Lots of monks, nuns and vicars become ghosts. So always look in churches and convents. Nuns and monks wear flapping garments for most of their lives so they are well equipped when they die. Listen for their chilling chant as they float about the cloisters a little above the cold stone floors, telling their beads.

As well as being snobbish, spooks tend to be set in their ways – they always remain at the level they knew. This only presents problems when the floor level rises rather than falls over the centuries and we witness the phenomenon of the footless ghost.

# Ghostly Habits

Mother Superior. & (floats higher than the other sisters.)

A pair of holy ghosts

Father O'Flaherty fresh from the flames of hell.

Straying balls are a constant nuisance.

# Transports to Terror

You are walking alone along a country road. It is dark and silent,
except for the rustle of horse chestnut leaves and the thud of a
falling conker. Suddenly you hear the thunder of hooves, the jangle
of a harness, the creaking of coach wheels. Can this be the last bus?

Cold and tired you get out the fare, but DO NOT press your silver
into the conductor's icy hand. Do not be tempted. For no-one
returns from a lift in the headless coachman's carriage.

# Hunting the Haunting

Are you brave? Could you sit in a dark cold crypt full of scuttling spiders, with slimy things slithering across the floor and gruesome ghouls moaning and groaning and dragging their chains and creeping up behind you. If so, spook spotting is for you.

Apart from nerves and guts all you need is a pig or cat and a few essential aids.

Pen with ink – Ghosts like writing messages

Candle in holder and lots of matches * ✗

Ball of string to find your way out of haunted houses.

* Ghosts love blowing candles out.

Egors a Sissy.

Typical Ghost message.

Spook Spotter's Guide.

Apparitions to Zombies

Successful photo of spook.

Lots of humbugs – Spooks favourite sweets.

# The O'Gools

Ghosts never move. They haunt the places in which they lived. The O'Gools are typical. They try not to disrupt the nice people who now live in their house but every so often one of them slips up and gets seen. Screams, tears, terror – if only the living knew how harmless these ghosts are:

For a start there's Dad, Mr Fingal Drool O'Gool, once a head teacher but a shadow of his former self. Then there's Mummy, Ginny O'Gool, whose fondness for spirits is famous, the older children Ralph the Wraith and Mona the moaner, the identically ghastly twins, Float and Gloat, and the pets Hairy and Scary.

Mummy and Daddy teach the young ones how to haunt without hurting. But Ralph and Mona enjoy throwing on a sheet and shocking half the neighbourhood. It's hard to keep them home at nights. Even the pets like to pop up in unexpected places and petrify the population.

"There's a poo in the loo, it must be you."

Float       Gloat

# High Fibre Diet

At night, when the real family have gone to bed, the O'Gools materialize for breakfast. They need building up to keep fit for haunting. Like ghosts themselves, ghost food has no substance and does not comply with the law of gravity.

Nor, under the influence of the children, does the furniture. Ghosts learn to levitate when they are very young and making other objects rise into the air is the favourite game of spook children. Objects flying about a room like frisbies are usually the work of undisciplined young spooks. The O'Gools never allow their children to play such games.

'Breakfast each night
Keeps a ghost ghostie
white.'
(Old ghost proverb.)

# Work for Weirdos.

Shh!

At midnight it is time for work. Some places have to be haunted and Mr O'Gool, for one, would never let people down. He and Hairy clock in on the stroke of twelve every night.

Dog's Delight

Every dog has his night and tonight is mine!

The Haunting Hound.

Shh!!
Silence is essential for a successful haunting.

Mona  Ralph

Daddy

Hairy
really has disappeared

Ralph and Mona follow their father for a bit of fiendish fun. They practise uncanny screams and demonic laughs – but still fail to frighten anyone.

'They haven't the knack,' says their father, Fingal the Fearsome Phantom. He does not have high hopes for his children.

# Hooligans a haunting

Mona and Ralph spend all night trying to distress the neighbours, ringing doorbells, tapping at windows, turning over dustbins. But it has no effect. People have grown used to things that go bump in the night. Nothing surprises them. Even the dogs and cats aren't scared of the two young ghouls. They might just as well have gone to school and learnt a bit from their elders.

## A Haunting Song
Listen in the dark, listen in the dark
Cats wailing, dogs barking
Dustbins flying, doors banging
Floorboards creaking, taps dripping
Ghosts lurking, ghosts slipping
Silently through the night.

Crying
Cockles
and
mussels

# A Night of Toils

With her husband gone a hauntin', Ginny is left at home
to play the role of bored houseghost. Light fingered, she
tinkles a rag on the grand piano while the hoover and the
broom and the duster dance in appreciation. Housework
is a hoot. She is a spook with a sparkle, a spectre with
splendour.

Meanwhile, Dad is hard at it, nose to the tombstone. In a
moment of weakness, he's left his job of haunting the
school and is down in the graveyard with a crowd of
disreputable, disembodied unearthly beings – his best
friends.

# Grave Matters

It's tomb opening at the local cemetery.

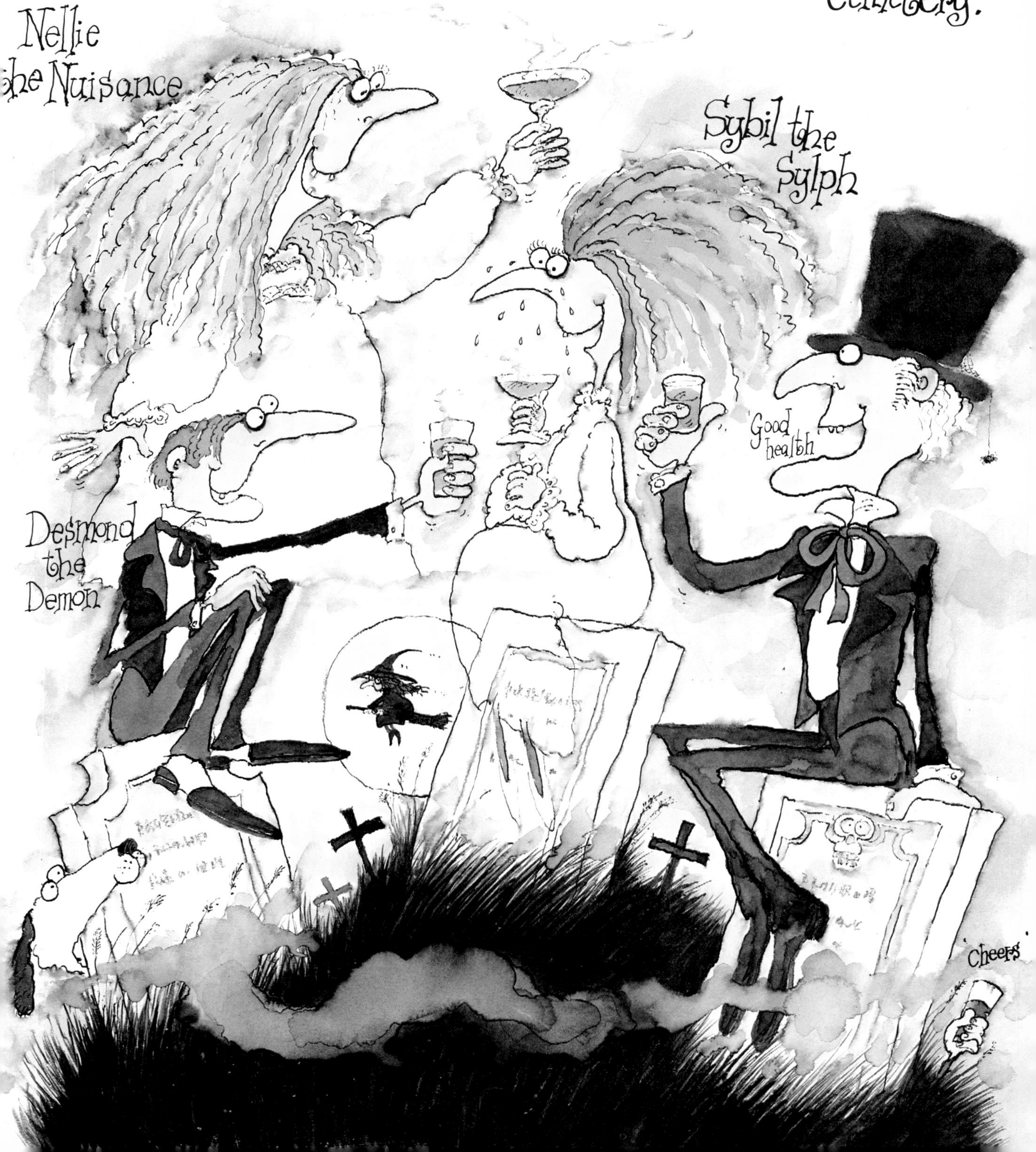

When Dad rolls home, he kisses his wife (and misses), tells Ralph and Mona they are too bad at haunting to miss a single night at school, tells Float and Gloat they are too young to disappear under his nose and upbraids Hairy and Scary for making themselves so scarce. Then he eats his supper and stands up, the better to tell them a ghost story. The Pie-Eyed Piper of Hamelin is their favourite. 'Once there was this piper . . .

.... hypnotised by the piper,

the rats danced themselves to death but this did not stop them bopping. Their ghosts dance on for ever and ever and ever . . . . .

And at the end of the night the O'Gools say their prayers for the living and disappear. They float into a small iron box, bolt its door and wait for night to come again. If you find a locked box in your house do not try to open it.

You never know what will come out.

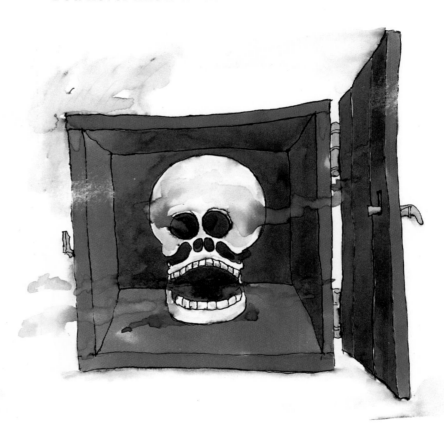

*Beware the lonely road, beware the dark forest, beware the gloomy cave, for here lurks ... the beast; hairy of leg, hairy of face, foul of breath, shambling and loping of gait, sharp in tooth and claw, beware the creature of darkness!*

A good description you might think of lots of things that go bump in the night, but this ancient text relates to creatures that are always described in hushed tones as gigantic, fearsome, dangerous and wicked. Sometimes green and slimy with long squirming tongues; sometimes soft and squidgy with four eyes, six legs, and spitting poison and sometimes coming from outer space: they are **MONSTERS!**
In this book we will explore the world of the monster. Who were they? Do they still exist? Where do they live? Do they have any friends? What and whom do they eat? Which are the worst monsters? Do you know a monster? All these and many more monstrous questions will be answered.

\* Typical monster greeting.

Woodsman Lore:- All they monsters ave an 'airy belly. Their feet ave huge and 'orribly 'orribly smelly!

# Hairy, Scary and BIG

Do you know of anyone with big hairy feet?

30 inches (or 4 x the width of this page)

Huge hairy monsters with enormous feet live in the forests of Canada and America. They are called 'Big Foot' or 'Sasquatch' by the native Americans. In 1924 Albert Ostman was carried off by a Big Foot while he was camping, though luckily he managed to escape. He reported that the creature was about three metres tall, covered in reddish brown hair and had very big smelly feet.

In Tibet they call the hairy giant the 'Yeti' or 'Abominable Snowman'. It lives high up in the Himalayan mountains. *

The Australians call their monster the 'Yowie'.

Ranger lore:–

> *The Yowie likes a booze*
> *An' then he has a snooze.*

\* You'd have to be sly to see a Yeti pass by
They live way up high and are very very shy.
(old sherpa rhyme)

Howie Yowie!

Good on ya Roo!

A werewolf* is a terrifying sight: have you seen a man transformed into a ferocious wolf every full moon? There are several signs by which a werewolf can be recognised. Take a good look around you. Do you see anyone with eyebrows that meet in the middle, with small pointed ears, sharp fingernails and, the surest sign of all, hairs on the palms of the hands?

# Beware Werewolves

Are you weird enough to become a werewolf? If you are—there are various methods you can try.

*It's working.*

Roll in the sand at full moon.

*Mmm.. Mmm..*

*Give me a bite.*

Eats wolfbane sandwiches for packed lunch or supper

Drink from the same water as a wolf.

(Perhaps you could let us know if any of these work.)

St Patrick cursed an Irish family who had upset him. They became werewolves every seven years for seventy years.

A curse on yee!

Grrrr! Grrr!

Not a silver bullet.

It was rumoured that King John was a werewolf. Norman monks heard sounds coming from his grave. They dug him up and re-buried him in unconsecrated ground.

? ?

Wooooooooo! Wooooooooo!

King John was a hairy fellow, with teeth long and yellow. His breath was smelly and really foul and every night you'd hear him howl.

Werewolves are hairy and very scary.

The werewolf can be defeated by taking three drops of its blood, while it is still in wolf form. An easier remedy is to shoot the wolf with a silver bullet. Or if you know his human name call it out loudly three times. Failing all these – RUN!

* Wer – Old English for man hence werewolf.

# Sea Monsters

Mon Dieu

In all the seas of the world dwell terrible, tentacled, squirming sea monsters and slippery, spitting sea serpents. They are the terror and torment of all those who sail the seven seas.

One of the largest sea-serpents ever encountered met the Bishop of Uppsala in Sweden in 1555. He described it as a very big serpent indeed, at least sixty metres in length and some six metres round with a mane of red hair.*

In November 1861, the crew of the French ship Electon battled with a huge sea creature. The monster eventually made off leaving behind an eight metre length of its tail.

*Possibly Scottish or Viking serpent.

How do you suppose when a serpent grows?
He tickles his toes and picks his nose?
No one knows.

In the dark and gloomy mist a sea serpent hissed...

I've just eaten up my brother. Now I'll go and eat up mother.

Old mariner lore:-
Seaweed on the shore monsters will roar.

When the sea surfs white monsters will bite.

# Watery, Weird and Warty

The best known of all the water monsters is Nessie of Loch Ness in Scotland. She is a dreadful, slimy, slithering Scottish reptile* with a long eel-like neck, enormous jaws and powerful flippers. Nessie emerges from the deep dark dank waters of Loch Ness to prey on American tourists who wear the wrong tartan.

In ancient times this terrible beast would drag foolhardy, hairy Scottish swimmers down into the dark waters of the Loch never to be seen again. However, in 565 St Columba commanded Nessie to be a 'Good Beastie' and thereafter she was, and left the swimmers alone (as far as we know).

In 1934, one moonlit night, a student called Arthur Grant was riding home, when he nearly ran into Nessie on his motorbike as she was crossing the road back to the Loch.

*Possibly a plesiosaur.

Most gigantic of all sea monsters is the Kraken. It is often as much as one and a half miles long and frequently mistaken for an island.

Possibly the squashiest of the water monsters are the 'Globsters', shapeless warty humps of green flesh covered in hair. They are found on Australian beaches and are often called Bruce or Sheila. If they are trodden on they can be very dangerous especially if they go bright red.

There once was a gorilla called King Kong
Who was so very big and strong
He went for a walk and arrived in New York
And caused the most monstrous Ding-Dong!

# Movie Monsters 1

Monsters are enthusiastic movie goers. They often go to the cinema to watch themselves on the big screen. They stuff themselves with monster-size buckets of popcorn, suck and slurp ice lollies, and guzzle big cokes. Have you ever sat behind anyone like that?

Movie Monster lore:– *Scrunch, gobble gobble slurp. It all ends in a burp.*

Favourite monster movies are:–

'The Creature from the Black Lagoon'
'The Beast from 1,000 Fathoms'
'The Abominable Snowman'
'The Thing from Outer Space'
'The Other Thing from Outer Space'
'Jaws'
'Alien'
'Godzilla'
'The Blob'

Hollywood has had many famous monster movie stars like King Kong the Giant gorilla. He terrified New York searching for his true love, the fair Fay Wray.

The Blob is a jelly-like monster that blobbed and gobbled everything in its path, becoming bigger and bigger. This film has lots of sticky moments.

Frankenstein's monster stepping out for two chilli and tuna and cheese and pepperoni take-away pizzas.

# Movie Monsters 2

A nutty old German scientist called Dr Frankenstein was a do-it-yourself maniac. He built his dream castle on the Rhine as a bolt hole, then made his own monster with bits and pieces he dug up. Frankenstein's monster was a simple but kindly fellow with a screw loose.

Slurp! Suck!

!!!!

I wonder why I'm a fly? I don't chew the way you do I just suck. Yuk!

'The Fly' is a horror film about a scientist who is half human, half housefly. This was caused by a fly getting into a teletransportation pod with the scientist. The result of this molecule mix-up was monstrous.

Dr Jeckyll drank a potent potion which turned him into the gruesome Mr Hyde. Mr Hyde was a monster with superhuman strength; he could see in the dark, had hairs on his chest, long white teeth and curly hair. Does your mum offer you potent potions and say, 'it'll put hairs on your chest'? Beware.

Heh! Heh! Heh! Heh! Heh!

...See old Jeckyll's been mixing his drinks again.

Yah! Bad show, what?

When space monsters glow    it's time to go.

# Space Monsters

In 1952 in Virginia, USA, a group of friends investigating a bright flashing light on a hillside, were chased by a huge, floating, glowing space monster with bulging eyes and long tentacle-like fingers.

Space monsters are reported to have visited earth for thousands of years. In 1961 Joe Somontan of Wisconsin, USA, was visited in his back garden by little green men. They gave him a pancake, and said that it was their mission to seek out New Worlds, to go where no little green men had gone before and to start an Intergalactic Pancake Delivery Service.

Some space monsters are not so friendly. In 1954 a lorry driver in Venezuela stopped in surprise to see a strange unearthly craft hovering over the road. Small, hairy monsters with glowing eyes emerged from the spacecraft and attacked the lorry driver. He was then thrown over four metres through the air. Since then the lorry driver has been wary of the small and hairy.

# Stranger than Strange

Deep in the jungles of Madagascar grows a tree with long tendrils covered in sharp spines. Its branches reach out and entwine unsuspecting picnickers, their cheese and tomato sandwiches and their smoky bacon crisps. Once snared, its victims are dragged into its dark heart never to be seen again. Never sit under this tree, it is the 'Man-Eating Tree of Madagascar'.*

*In ancient times Madagascar was known as the Land of the Man-Eating Trees.

In Géranden, France between the years of 1764 and 1767 the countryside was plagued by a wild beast. It was bright red, covered in scales, with a mouth the size of a lion. It was the terror of the local shepherds, carrying off sheep, tourists and croissants at every opportunity.

Isuchi-Gumo is a Japanese Goblin Spider with the terrifying ability to enlarge its horrible, hairy body at night. Could this be the original Little Miss Muffet?

# Monstrous Meals

## Monster Menus

### ~ Breakfast ~

Vile Bile Juice (orange or lemon)
Weetabits (crunchy, wholesome bits of anything)
Cold, lumpy porridge (for the hairy, hardy monster)
Snap, Crackle & Belch (to wake you up in the morning)
Musheli (for the healthy monster) containing dried maggots,
yoghurt coated beetles, dried worms and lice flakes
Boiled Bad Eggs with toasted fingers (dip and crunch)

### ~ Snacks ~

Blood Oranges
Yeti Yoghurt
Smoky Bogie flavoured crisps

Monsters are greedy gobblers, they believe in making a meal out of every meal time.
They shove enormous quantities of food into their ever open, vast,
dribbling jaws.  Monster manners are dreadful.

## ~ Lunch ~

Snot Sandwiches with granary bread
Giant Giblet Burger (charcoal grilled)
Sliced Snake Salad
Snail and Salad Cream Sandwich
Tripe in warm milk (for the sickly monster)
Hot Thick Sick Soup (for the cold monster)
Croque Monstère

## ~ High Tea ~

Vomit Vol-Au-Vents
Snottage Rolls
Green Gilbert Gateau
Snail Slime Sponge Cake

## ~ Dinner ~

Spit Soup
Shepherd Pie (made with three fresh shepherds)
Toad-in-the-hole with mashed maggots
Fried fingers with chips
Hot Potty Pie with Fried Lice
Squashed Fly Pie
Mucus Mousse
Green Mould Jelly with Frozen Eyes Cream

They slurp soup, chew with their mouths open, lick their plates, eat with their paws and put their elbows on the table. They never say 'please', 'thank you' or 'excuse me'. And they always burp.

# Monsters at Work

Even monsters need to earn an honest crust. Some professions have more monster appeal than others. Many monsters are attracted to teaching.

They often reach the top as headmasters or headmistresses, commanding respect mingled with terror.

You horrible little monster!

Yes, sir.

Get off the grass!!

Park keeping appeals to monsters. It is a healthy out-of-doors occupation with plenty of exercise, and the opportunity to meet lots of children.

Eeeeeeek!

Werewolves make dedicated night watchmen. They are physically well suited for this job as they can see in the dark and move silently.

Children who have nannies remember them well after they are grown up. This is not surprising as lots of nannies are monsters. Hairy monsters make super nannies as babies love to cuddle into their hairy chests.
Nanny lore:–

Nanny knows best
You'll get a cold on the chest
Just put on a vest
Nanny knows best.

I love my Nanny, she's so weird, especially when she shaves her beard, she really thinks it's such a lark to race me madly round the park.

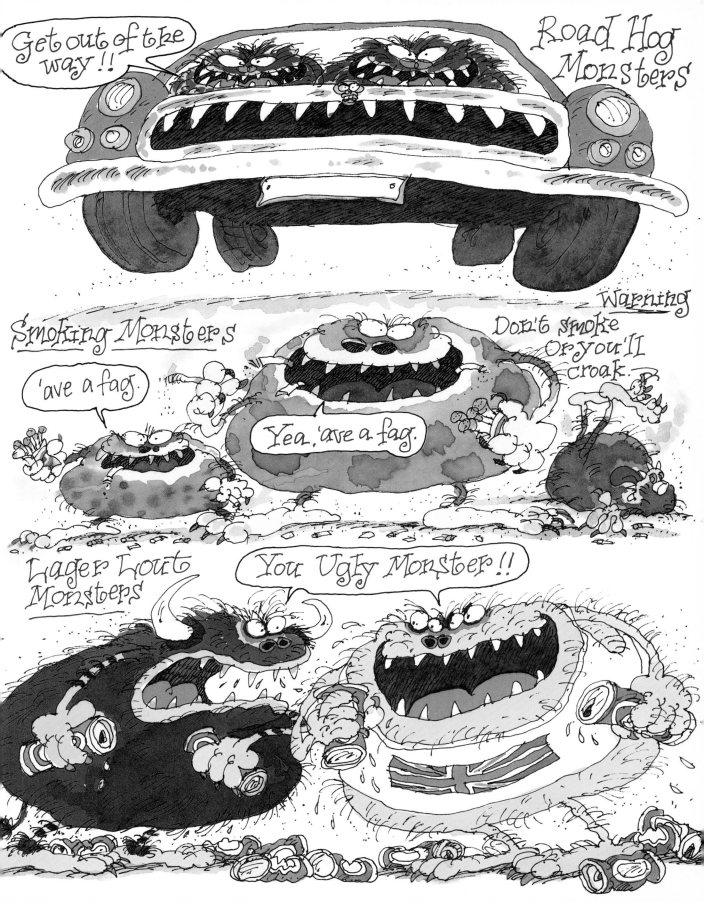

# Monstrous Old Jokes

Monsters love to cackle and titter.
Here are a few old belly laughs and rib-ticklers.

# Monster Rhymes

This little monster went to market.
This little monster stayed at home.
This little monster had roast beef.
This little monster had none, And this little monster went wee..wee... all the way home.

Wee...wee...wee...

Monday's monster's fair of face

Aren't I pretty?

Pom! Pom!

Tuesday's monster's full of grace.

Wednesday's monster's full of woe.

woe woe woe

I've a long way to go!

Thursday's monster's got far too go.

I love you, have my best bone

Oh, thank you.

Friday's monster is loving and giving.

Saturday's monster works hard for his living.

It's hard work but I like it.

But the monster that is born on the sabbath day is bonny blithe* good and gay.*

I'm so bonny.

I'm so happy.

I'm so good.

Hee! Hee!

*Blithe: Old monster for happy   *Gay: Old monster for greeful.

It is said that
any monster bits that
are chopped off a monster
will re-form into
a complete monster
again.
You have been warned.